FRANZESKA G. EWART

Under the Spell of
Bryony Bell

First published 2005 by
A & C Black Publishers Ltd
37 Soho Square, London, W1D 3QZ

www.acblack.com

ISBN 0-7136-7172-6

A CIP catalogue for this book is available from the British Library.

A&C Black uses paper produced with elemental chlorine-free
pulp, harvested from managed sustained forests.

Printed and bound in Great britain by CPD Wales, Ebbw Vale

FRANZESKA G. EWART

Under the Spell of Bryony Bell

Illustrated by Kelly Waldek

A & C Black • London

For my music teacher, Eileen Silcocks

One

Bryony Bell braced herself against her dressing table. Under her breath she whispered, 'Geronimo!' Then she pushed off and, with one leg stretched out behind her, glided across her bedroom, her Viper 3000 rollerskates cutting a perfectly straight swathe through the pink shagpile carpet.

From her open window the sounds of *The Singing Bells'* daily practice wafted up from the Music Studio, but Bryony deafened her ears to the air-rending round of scales and arpeggios. She had more important things to think about.

'Left foot take-off,' she muttered, leaning sideways to balance on her two outside wheels. 'Bend the knee … arms out … and … UP!'

She launched herself into the air and, just as she felt her head bounce off the light fitting, snapped her arms round her waist and went into what – with any luck – would be a triple spin. The alarm clock on her bedside table bounced into the air as she landed and, checking her final position in the wardrobe mirror, she caught it neatly, replaced it, then curtsied in its direction.

'Two-and-a-half turns in the air,' she smiled. 'Almost there!'

Bryony skated back over to the dressing table and prepared to try again, when a particularly ear-splitting series of chords rang out. She sighed and closed the window.

There was never a moment's silence in the house any more. Ever since Mum's brainchild, *The Singing Bells*, had won a recording contract and £50,000, there was no stopping the little 'uns. All the younger children – Angelina, the twins Melody and Melissa, and little Emmy-Lou, practised every single day. Even Little Bob Bell, who was hardly potty-trained, kept time with his rattle and was showing a remarkable sense of rhythm.

It was hard, Bryony reflected – and not for the first time – being the only non-singing Bell apart from Big Bob. And since fame had hit his household, her dad had had no time to worry about his lack of musical talent. He had been too busy putting his carpentry skills to good use building an extension.

Not that Bryony begrudged *The Singing Bells* their success. She always practised her rollerskating routines to their CD, *The Singing Bells Sing the Blues*. Her bedroom walls were festooned with publicity posters featuring Clarissa with her blondest, most luxurious hairstyles and wearing her slinkiest, sparkliest evening dresses, and the little 'uns, in matching colours but rather trendier styles, behind her.

She kept all their press cuttings too – photographs of Angelina being interviewed on the children's TV programme *Meet The Starlets*; Melissa's Hair Tips column in *Girlie* magazine; Melody and Emmy-Lou modelling in Kute Kids clothes catalogue; even Little Bob sitting on his potty advertising the latest brand of plastic knickers...

But Bryony had to admit guiltily that she sometimes wished *The Singing Bells* had not become so famous. Or that they would find a way to let her be famous with them. For if anyone was destined for stardom; if anyone had talent and charisma, not to mention the coolest, sleekest pair of skating boots in the entire Universe, it was Bryony Bell. OK, so she couldn't sing – but she had razzmatazz in bucketloads!

Bryony took a deep breath. You had to look on the bright side, she told herself sternly. After all, *The Singing Bells'* fame had its advantages. The Music Studio, which was part of Big Bob's extension, was pretty cool. At least she didn't have to worry that her window was going to shatter when Clarissa hit her famous top 'C', and her walls didn't vibrate when the latest Bell Family Song was sung. And occasionally she was even allowed to skate on its polished pine floor.

Big Bob peeked in. At the sight of her dad, Bryony perked up. 'Did you hear my landing?' she asked.

Big Bob nodded. 'Just as well I reinforced your floorboards, Bryony lass,' he winked. 'So – did you make the triple?'

'Cat's whisker away from it,' Bryony told him cheerfully. 'But it's keeping the concentration going…' She glanced towards the window and Big Bob put his arm round her shoulders.

'I know, lass,' he said sympathetically. 'Tell you what, though – it's worse in the potting shed. Sometimes I wonder if that's what's doing for my geranium cuttings.'

Right on cue, the air was split by a rousing rendition of the Bell Family Song. Since their rise to fame, Clarissa had rewritten it. It was now sung with American accents and a great deal of whooping; and it always gave Bryony a strange, hollow feeling in the pit of her stomach.

We're the Singing Bells, the song rang out,
And we made it to the top
But the Singing Bells
Sure ain't never gonna stop
For the Singing Bells're
Gonna grow 'n' grow in fame…
Till THE BROADWAY BELLS
What? The BROADWAY *Bells?*
Yes, the B-R-O-A-D-W-A-Y BELLS
IS
    OUR
        NAME!'

'And that's that,' said Big Bob. 'It's Broadway or bust, I'm afraid.'

Bryony swallowed hard. The pit of her stomach felt hollower than usual.

'Why Broadway, Dad?' she asked at last. 'Why the Broadway Bells?'

Big Bob sighed and sat down on Bryony's bed. She perched on his little lap. 'What's wrong with here?' she asked, wobbling slightly.

'It's the glamour of it, Bryony,' Big Bob answered. 'Every performer dreams of going to New York and starring on Broadway. All the biggest theatres are there. Your mum's always had what you call a 'burning ambition', and nothing's going to quench the flames.'

'It's just…' Bryony stopped. She couldn't say it. It was too selfish for words.

Big Bob finished her sentence. 'It's just that, when they fly off to America, the house is going to be kind of empty with just the two of us?' he said. 'Is that what's worrying you?'

Bryony bit her lip. 'It's one of the things, Dad.'

'Come on, spit it out.' Big Bob bobbed his knees, as if to bounce the words out of her.

'Well,' Bryony began slowly, 'before *The Singing Bells* got famous, they said I could be in the act too, skating while they sang, but…' She stuck out her feet and they both surveyed the magnificent, glistening-white Viper 3000s in silence.

Neither needed to say it. Every time Bryony asked if she could be part of a new routine, it seemed one of *The Singing Bells* came up with all sorts of reasons why she shouldn't. When they had done the Winter Wonderland Christmas Spectacular and Bryony had longed to be an ice-skater in the background, Angelina had put a spoke in her Ice-Lite wheel.

'I don't think Bryony should skate behind us,' she had said, shaking her head so that the beads on her braids ricocheted off one another like gunfire. 'I think it'll take the audience's attention away from the music...'

The same had happened when they had sung a medley of Easter songs and Bryony had begged to be allowed to put on an Easter Bunny costume and skate around the audience, distributing Easter eggs.

'I think having an Easter Bunny is childish,' Angelina had piped up. 'specially an Easter Bunny on skates. Bunnies,' she had added, warming to her theme, 'don't glide. Bunnies hop. I know that 'cause I used to keep rabbits when I was young,' she had concluded.

Bryony sighed. Angelina was always putting obstacles in her way.

'Tell you what, Bryony,' Big Bob said suddenly. 'Why don't you get out your Swan costume – give it a bit of a burl?'

With a bound, Bryony sprang off Big Bob's lap, opened the wardrobe door and, very carefully, brought out the shimmering, silvery-white costume. She held its feathery skirt up to her cheek and buried her nose in it, breathing in the sweet smell of success.

'Remember the Swan Dance, Dad?' she said, smiling broadly at the memory of her music teacher, Mrs Quigg's, wonderful play, The Ugly Duckling in which she had starred – not only in the title role, but also as the Swan in all its glory.

'Could I ever forget it, princess? You were magic!'

Bryony held the Swan costume to her chest and looked at herself in the mirror. The silver-sequined swan on the bodice sparkled back at her, and her pert bunches with their lily-of-the-valley hair ties stood triumphantly upright like victory flags. Hope flooded back, and she beamed at Big Bob.

'I've got star quality, Dad,' she told him decisively. 'They're bound to find an opening for me soon. Then I'll go to Broadway too.'

Big Bob ran the toe of his boot along the shagpile. 'Actually, Bryony,' he said quietly, 'your mum's had a bit of news. I'm not supposed to say, though.'

Bryony frowned. 'Oh go on, Dad,' she said. 'I promise I won't let on.'

But Big Bob shook his head. 'More than my life's worth,' he said. 'Let's just say there's a project in the pipeline and...'

'A project that needs a Class 'A' skater?'

From below, a crescendo of sound rose to fill the room as the massed voices of *The Singing Bells* resonated round the garden in a lusty chorus of 'It's time for tea!' in the key of 'G'.

Big Bob detached Bryony from his knee and stood up. 'Neglecting my post,' he said. 'Should've had the kettle on by now.'

'Does it?' Bryony insisted, but Big Bob was clumping downstairs, hell for leather.

'Come and butter the muffins, princess,' he called back up at her. 'Then all will be revealed!'

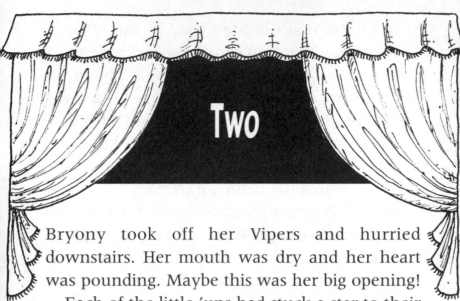

TWO

Bryony took off her Vipers and hurried downstairs. Her mouth was dry and her heart was pounding. Maybe this was her big opening!

Each of the little 'uns had stuck a star to their bedroom door and, as always, Bryony counted them longingly on her way past. One for Melody, one for Melissa, a slightly smaller one for Emmy-Lou, and – predictably – a huge, mega-sparkly one for Angelina. Even Little Bob had a rather-badly coloured-in red one.

Five stars. How long would it be before there were six?

In the living room, the little 'uns were sitting stiffly on the settee with Clarissa, clad from head to toe in a leopard-skin catsuit, standing in front of them. She had a piece of paper in her hand and as Bryony came in she gave her a little frown.

'Sorry, Mum,' Bryony muttered. 'I'll just get the—'

'Later, Bryony,' Clarissa said crisply. 'This is no time for muffins. I have an important announcement to make.'

Bryony perched on the arm of the settee beside Angelina. She tried to catch her sister's eye but Angelina stared straight ahead, the strands of her braids forming a bead curtain between them.

'I have a contract,' Clarissa announced. There was a ripple of expectation, which Clarissa quickly quelled. 'Before you get too excited,' she said, 'I'll tell you – it's not Broadway. It is the Empress Theatre.'

'The Empress Theatre?' Angelina repeated, giving her braids a disdainful toss. 'We're not doing Summer Panto, are we?'

'What happened to "Broadway or bust"?' Melissa chipped in, her voice whinier than usual and her new Afro curls bristling with indignation.

'There's nothing wrong with Summer Panto,' Clarissa said. 'Think of it as a chance to get noticed for our acting as well as our singing.'

'Do people get noticed at the Empress Theatre?' Melody asked doubtfully.

'Of course they do,' Clarissa replied. 'That's where all the big American talent scouts hang out! There's every chance we'll be headhunted, and then…'

She slapped her knees three times, and waited till the little 'uns had done the same. Then she raised her hands and, in time to more knee-slapping, began to chant:

It's Broadway or bust!
It's Broadway or bust!
Whatever we do,
Wherever we go,
It's Broadway or bust!

All the little Bells clapped and sang jubilantly, and Little Bob's face turned crimson as he bounced up and down and joined in. For some time now, Melissa had been trying to explain to him that it was 'Broadway', and not 'Bobway', but he still preferred his own version and sang it loud and clear at every opportunity.

Soon everyone was talking excitedly about the Summer Panto, which ran in the Empress Theatre during the summer months alongside a variety show. This year it was to be *Cinderella* and Clarissa was explaining, with much slapping of her thigh, that she would be playing Prince Charming.

'And you will be my chorus,' she said, as Big Bob tiptoed in with a plate heaped high with butter-shiny muffins. For a while the Bells chewed in silence. Only Bryony's muffin remained untouched. She was watching Big Bob. He looked, she thought, rather sad. And when Big Bob was sad, so was Bryony.

'There's something else,' Clarissa went on. 'We get to write the songs. So we need to come up with some sure-fire show stoppers! Now – anything you want to ask?'

The little Bells shot question after question at Clarissa.

'Will we get to sing solos?'

'Will we have a suite of star dressing rooms?'

'Will there be any famous soap stars?'

'Will Little Bob get a bit part?'

Still Bryony sat, butter dribbling down her arm.

'I think Bryony has something she wants to know,' Big Bob said at last.

A big lump formed in Bryony's throat, but she said as casually as she could, 'So – is there an opening for an ace skater in this Panto?'

Everyone stopped talking. Angelina glanced sideways at her. It was just a tiny glance, but it spoke volumes.

'Oh, Bryony,' Clarissa said at last. She was smiling, but her diamante earrings swayed as she shook her head. 'I'm not sure. I mean, what part could you play on skates?'

Bryony thought frantically.

'Well…' she began. 'I could be… I could be the Fairy Godmother! I could come gliding in, with a sparkly frock and a magic wand, and I could change the pumpkin into a coach…'

Clarissa looked thoughtful. 'Y-es,' she said slowly. 'But I had a kind of notion that maybe Angelina could play the part. She's got great rhythm, and her high kicks are brilliant. Given me a cracking idea for a Fairy Godmother song.'

'It'd be really magical, though,' Big Bob put in, 'if Bryony skated on. Wouldn't it?'

He looked at the six Bell faces hopefully, and the six Bell faces looked silently back at him. Angelina's lower lip curled into the deepest pout she could muster.

'Wouldn't it?' he repeated.

* * *

'So that's it,' Bryony concluded. 'Seems like I will not be going to the Ball.'

It was the next day after school, and Bryony was sitting on the wall of Peachtree Primary. On the pavement below, gazing up at her with huge sorrowful eyes, was her best friend Abid Ashraf.

'I think it's criminal,' Abid said for the fourth time. 'There you are, bursting with talent, and they're not giving you a look-in. Well, they don't know what they're missing, if you ask me.'

Bryony brightened up. Abid could always be depended upon to say just the right thing at the right time.

'"C'est la vie", as Mrs Quigg says,' she sighed. Then she jumped off the wall, laced up her everyday black skates, and skated round behind Abid. 'Maybe,' she said, brightening up, 'they'll have a change of heart and find a skate-on part for me after all.

'Come on, Abid,' she said, giving him a push. 'If we step on it, we could see the first rehearsal!' And she steered Abid round in the direction of the Empress Theatre.

The main theatre doors were shut, but Bryony skated in through the Stage Door. From the bowels of the theatre, voices rang out.

'There they are!' Bryony hissed. 'And they don't sound very pleased.'

The Singing Bells sounded anything but pleased. Above a series of aggrieved little cries, Clarissa's voice boomed loud, strong and very, very upset. Then a door burst open and out she marched, her face red and tear-streaked.

'Mum?' said Bryony. 'What's wrong?'

She squeezed her mother's arm comfortingly, and Clarissa dabbed her eyes with a lace-trimmed handkerchief. 'Oh ... nothing really, Bryony,' she sniffed. 'They've double-booked the stage – some audition or other – and it's going to delay our first rehearsal. Sorry, love,' she went on, pulling herself together. 'I'm overwrought. It's the last thing the little 'uns need...' And she shepherded them into a cramped and dowdy-looking dressing room.

Bryony pushed Abid back down the corridor. 'Let's go, Abid,' she said, adding under her breath, 'Seems like the "suite of star dressing rooms" didn't materialise...'

She was about to open the stage door when a voice crackled through the tannoy system.

'And now, ladies and gentlemen, let's hear it for Ken Undrum – Man of Mystery!'

There was a short drumroll, then silence.

Bryony listened, skating her way slowly back into the theatre followed by a bemused-looking Abid.

'What is it, Bryony?' he hissed, as Bryony led him to the wings of the Empress Theatre stage itself.

Bryony parted the red velvet curtain and peered at the little man with the huge red handlebar moustache who was standing in the spotlight.

'Sssh!' she told Abid. 'Just watch…'

Ken Undrum, Man of Mystery, took off his top hat to reveal a shock of faded red hair, and placed it on the table in front of him. Then he raised his wand and, muttering mysteriously under his breath, gave the hat's rim three gentle taps.

'Oh my!' gasped Bryony, clutching her cheeks in wonder at what happened next. It was, she thought, the most awesome, the most spectacular, thing she had ever seen.

Suddenly an idea began to take shape in Bryony's mind. Perhaps there were other ways of getting that star on her bedroom door…

Three

Bryony shook Abid's sleeve excitedly. 'Are you thinking what I'm thinking, Abid?' she said.

'I'm thinking there are an awful lot of white rabbits on that stage,' replied Abid hoarsely, 'and rabbit hair doesn't half go for my tubes. I can feel a wheeze starting...'

He sneezed three times, to demonstrate his asthma.

'I need to get out of here, Bryony. You know what I'm like with fur,' he said as he hurried off.

But Bryony could not tear herself away. Ken Undrum bowed at the three people auditioning him, and received a very small and unenthusiastic ripple of applause in return. One of the auditioners was writing something down on a clipboard. None, Bryony thought, looked impressed by the Man of Mystery's stupendous magic act.

The rabbits, meanwhile, were skipping slowly round the stage. A few nibbled at the curtain, and one particularly large one, its pink eyes gleaming with determination, gnawed at the base of the microphone. Ken watched them helplessly, finally deciding to leave them be.

'I shall now saw a lady in half,' he announced solemnly, wheeling a mirrored box into position and giving each of its sides a thwack with the blade of a saw. Bryony's heart skipped a beat. The danger of it all thrilled her to the core.

'My glamorous assistant is unfortunately indisposed,' Ken went on apologetically. 'So perhaps I could ask a member of the audience…'

He waved the saw seductively at the auditioning panel, who glared expressionlessly back at him. It was clear that nobody had the slightest intention of being sawn in half.

'Pity,' Ken said. 'Never mind, I will pass on to my next trick. I call it "Bread-on-a-Thread".'

He pushed a length of thread into his mouth and chewed. 'Now,' he said, in a muffled voice, 'prepare to be astounded…' and he began to pull the thread back out.

Bryony, leaning as far forward as she dared, could not believe her eyes. Incredibly, it was beaded with dollops of damp dough!

Unable to stop herself any longer, Bryony glided on to the stage, pirhouetted once round the mirrored box – carefully avoiding the rabbits

– then curtsied first to Ken and then to the auditioners.

'I'm Bryony Bell,' she told everyone. 'And you can saw me in half any day!'

Ken's dark little eyes lit up and his face crinkled into a grateful smile as he opened the lid. Bryony prepared to clamber in but before she could, the man with the clipboard stood up and said wearily, 'I'm sorry, Mr Undrum, but we can't have a minor being sawn in half.'

'Particularly a minor on roller skates,' the woman added.

'Perhaps,' the first man went on, 'if you were to re-audition when your glamorous assistant has recovered…?'

'To be perfectly honest,' the other man put in, 'your act simply isn't slick enough for our summer season. Good afternoon, Mr Undrum. Please ensure you have all your rabbits with you as you leave.'

Ken Undrum's whole body seemed to sag. He began to fold up the little table. Bryony, regretfully, took her foot back out of the box and skated to his side.

'Not slick enough,' Ken repeated, giving the table a shake. 'Not flipping slick enough!' A shower of white hairs glistened in the spotlight then sank floorwards. Ken turned to Bryony. His face was criss-crossed with wrinkles, like a walnut, and his blackberry eyes gleamed bright with disappointment.

'That phrase has dogged me all my life,' he sighed as he picked up the table and three of the rabbits. 'Dogged me,' he repeated, struggling offstage.

Bryony secured two rabbits under each arm and followed Ken down the corridor. Another lump was beginning to form in her throat, as she remembered how bad she had felt the day before.

'I thought you were magnificent, Mr Undrum,' she said sincerely.

Ken opened a dressing-room door and motioned to Bryony to go in. The room was tiny, every inch filled with cases and bags and boxes. Each surface heaved with silk scarves and playing cards and skittles and tiny white balls, and on top of everything a pyramid of ten rabbit hutches perched precariously. It was an Aladdin's Cave of magic, and Bryony was beside herself with admiration and wonder.

'What did you just say?' Ken asked, opening one of the hutches and gently placing two rabbits inside.

'Simply magnificent,' Bryony repeated. 'However did you make all those rabbits come out of your hat?'

Ken smiled bashfully. 'It's all in the the way you wave the wand,' he whispered, tapping the side of his nose.

'Really?' said Bryony.

Ken took a black-and-white wand out of his pocket and waved it. 'Magical wrist action,' he explained. 'Only given to the chosen few.'

'So you can't learn to do magic?' Bryony asked, suddenly deflated.

Ken thought about it. 'Well, yes,' he said, 'You can. If you've got someone to teach you how…' Then he took Bryony's rabbits from her, locked them away, and headed back to get the rest. Bryony trailed behind him.

'Will your glamorous assistant be better soon?' she asked. As soon as she had, she wished she hadn't.

'There is no glamorous assistant,' Ken told her, frowning. 'Left me for a knife-thrower.

Gets paid double to stand on a big bull's eye and get swords thrown at her five nights a week and twice on Saturdays.' He sighed deeply. 'I'm telling you, young lady – in this business, it's dog eat dog.'

They lifted the box together and Bryony balanced the five remaining white rabbits on top. Rather precariously, Ken and she struggled to the dressing room, where Abid was waiting. At the sight of the rabbits he coughed and backed away.

'This is Mr Undrum, Abid,' said Bryony. 'This is my friend Abid, Mr Undrum. He and I were just saying how much we'd love to have a magic act.'

She gave Abid a dig in the ribs with her elbow. 'Weren't we, Abid?'

'No,' said Abid, backing even further away as Bryony kicked the door open and the unmistakable scent of twenty rabbits and ten hutchfuls of soiled straw billowed out to meet him.

Bryony helped Ken put everything in place and, when the ten cages were filled, dusted herself down and said brightly, 'That's you, Mr Undrum. All ready for the road.'

Ken, however, did not move. He stood miserably, gazing around at the mass of equipment. Then he peered into the topmost hutch and stroked a quivering pink nose with his fingertip.

'Oh, Snowflake, what am I going to do?' he asked sorrowfully. 'No money, no assistant, no lodgings and, worst of all for you, my lad, no lettuce!'

Bryony opened her mouth to speak, but she was so choked with sympathy for Ken's plight that nothing came. She poked her head round the door. 'Your house is enormous, Abid,' she whispered pointedly.

Abid frowned and shook his head. 'Don't even go there, Bryony,' he said firmly. 'There is no way I am taking home twenty rabbits.'

Bryony nodded. Of course it was impossible. She thought again about how she had felt the day before, when no one had wanted her in the Panto act. Then she thought about the house, filled to bursting-point with Bells. No, it was quite, quite out of the question to bring anyone else home.

Ken was going from hutch to hutch, shoulders hunched, his mop of red hair hiding his face as he spoke reassuringly to each rabbit in turn.

'You know what the old song says, Lily my girl,' he muttered fondly to the huge rabbit that had almost felled the microphone. '"There's a rainbow round the corner..."'

Suddenly Bryony pictured Big Bob, admiring his newly planted vegetable patch. A few weeks from now it would be heaving with carrots and cabbages and lettuces. And wasn't he always complaining that the grass grew faster than he could cut it?

She took a deep breath and, ignoring Abid, who was shaking his head so hard his cheeks shone red, she put her arm round Ken's shoulders and said, 'Don't worry, Mr Undrum. You can move in with us. We've got a spare bedroom, and space in the potting shed for at least four hutches.'

And before Ken could say another word Bryony heaved a suitcase, a bundle of silk scarves, and a stack of tumblers into Abid's arms and, picking up two of the rabbit hutches, steered him triumphantly out of the Empress Theatre.

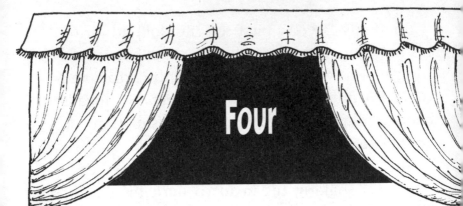

Four

'A lodger? Well, I must say, Bryony, you might have asked first.'

Clarissa poked her head back into the Music Studio, yelled, 'Last chorus again, and watch that B flat!', closed the door behind her and faced Bryony. You could have cut the air in the garden with a knife.

Bryony wheeled her Ice-Lite wheels back and forth on the path. If only her dad hadn't been on back shift. It would have been so much easier to have asked him...

'But, Mum,' she pleaded, 'we've got a spare bedroom. And I'll look after him, I promise. And help take care of his rab—'

She stopped in the nick of time. Clarissa shot her a look, her Emerald Lustre eye-shadow flashing suspiciously.

'He's got nowhere to go, Mum,' Bryony went on. 'He just needs somewhere till his luck changes. Pleeeeeease...'

Clarissa sighed. 'I don't know, Bryony, really I don't,' she said. 'I'll have to discuss it with your father. In the meantime, you'd better bring him in. Can't have him standing out in the street with his luggage.' And she began to march down the garden path.

Bryony spun round to skate backwards, clutching her by the shoulders. 'There's one other thing, Mum,' she said carefully. 'Mr Undrum has a few … props. He's a magician. He can do all sorts of brilliant magic. Oh, you and Dad are going to just love him!'

'Props?' Clarissa repeated. They had almost run out of path. In a moment, the true extent of Mr Undrum's stage equipment would be revealed.

'A few bits and pieces,' Bryony went on casually. She turned round and noted with relief that the full horror of the scene was momentarily blocked by Abid's large form.

'Abid thinks he's cool too,' Bryony added, giving him a look, and Abid obediently nodded and muttered a rather muted, 'Cool as anything, Mrs Bell.'

'And he so needs our help…' Bryony said, steering her mother round Abid and bracing herself. 'Mum,' she said steadily, 'meet Mr Ken Undrum, Man of Mystery.'

Dubiously, Clarissa stretched out her hand to

shake Mr Undrum's. As she did, her eyes narrowed as she scanned from packing case to packing case, finally alighting on the ten rabbit hutches. She froze, mid-shake.

Mr Undrum, however, seemed unabashed. 'Charmed to meet you, Mrs Bell,' he said, with a winning smile. 'It is not often that one stands in the presence of true greatness.' He looked Clarissa up and down approvingly. 'And, if I may make so bold, such exquisite beauty.'

Clarissa smoothed down her pink velour jumpsuit and fluttered her green eyelids. Then she looked back at the rabbit hutches. 'These are your … props, Mr Undrum?' she asked.

'Do please call me Ken,' Mr Undrum smiled. 'You know, Mrs Bell, I was just saying to your charming daughter, how rare it is to find a star whom fame has not tarnished. And you, dear lady, have shown such generosity of spirit towards a fellow thespian...' He sighed happily. 'I thank you from the very depths of my soul!'

And he lifted Clarissa's hand to his lips and gave it a tiny kiss.

Clarissa blushed. 'Call me Clarissa,' she said, glancing sheepishly at Bryony and Abid, 'and please walk this way.'

Triumphantly, Bryony gave Abid's sleeve a shake.

'One Bell down,' she thought as they heaved Ken's paraphernalia through the front door. 'Only six to go.'

* * *

By the time the little 'uns were called in to meet their new lodger, Ken's cases and boxes and hutches had been squeezed into the spare bedroom. Eight of the more resilient rabbits had been rehoused in Big Bob's potting shed on a shelf above his seed trays, and been left gazing longingly at the array of tiny vegetables sprouting tantalisingly beneath them.

Ken himself was looking magnificent in a deep-red, though distinctly threadbare, velvet jacket, and he had evidently doused himself in some very pungent aftershave, so when the little 'uns filed in, the atmosphere was overwhelmingly musky.

Bryony introduced each Bell in turn, and Ken kissed every hand – even Little Bob's. Little Bob loved it, and bounced up and down gurgling 'Bobway or bust!' very wetly. Then everyone sat, surveying the unexpected addition to the household over their teacups.

'I believe you are a magician?' Clarissa said.

'Indeed I am,' Ken said, inclining his head modestly. 'And perhaps, when we have finished our refreshments, the children would like to be astounded?'

Before you could say 'abracadabra' the Bells had polished off their tea and were sitting waiting, 'astound me' written all over their faces.

'If you will excuse me,' Ken said, 'I shall make ready.'

As soon as he had gone, everyone spoke at once.

'He looks ever so magical.'

'Doesn't half smell funny.'

'Has he got a real wand?'

'What'll Dad say?'

At the last question Clarissa gave Bryony a worried look, and Bryony passed the look on to Abid. She had a sudden picture of the eight rabbits drooling down at the seedtrays in the potting shed. The seedtrays that were Big Bob's pride and joy…

Then she gave herself a little shake. Dad would be fine. Dad was always fine.

It took Ken ages to prepare to astound the Bells, but eventually he swept in and everyone gasped at the sight of his black cloak with its red silk lining which, although rather frayed at the edges, gave him a very grand look.

'Would you look at that, Abid,' Bryony whispered admiringly. 'Mystery seeps from his very pores...' And she sat on the edge of the settee.

Ken raised his wand and did a few mid-air manouvres with it. Bryony watched, concentrating hard. It didn't look that difficult to master. Not unlike, in a way, learning a new skating move. Then, all of a sudden, Ken did something no one expected.

'Jeepers!' he said. 'Whad'ya think of this, kids?'

Bryony was suddenly puzzled. Wasn't that an American accent?

Ken had dropped onto his knees and was picking up something small and dark. He placed it carefully on the palm of his hand, then showed it to everyone. Clarissa looked mortified.

'What must you be thinking of us, Ken,' she said apologetically. 'A dead fly!'

'Think nothing of it, dear lady,' Ken said soothingly as he scanned round his spellbound audience. 'This most fortuitous find,' he breathed mysteriously, 'gives me the opportunity to demonstrate my incredible transcendental powers.'

There was a sharp intake of breath.

'Is that something to do with teeth?' Melissa whispered to Clarissa, who blushed and explained that it had nothing whatsoever to do with anything so ordinary. 'Powers of the mind,' she whispered. 'Everso impressive!'

'In just one moment,' Ken went on hypnotically, his red moustache trembling, 'you will see that I have power over life and death!'

There was an almost tangible quiver of excitement from the settee as Ken clasped the dead fly in his left hand, drew his wand from his pocket, and began to mutter mysteriously.

Bryony leant forward, straining to make out the spell. She was dying to ask him something. Eventually it was too much for her and she jumped to her feet.

'Please, Mr Undrum, may I wave the magic wand?'

For a moment Ken seemed about to pass her it, but then he shook his head apologetically. 'Better not,' he said. 'One false flick, and who knows what might appear?'

Bryony sat back down. Her disappointment, however, was soon forgotten as Ken stretched out his palm, and – sure enough – there was the fly, right as rain, rubbing its front legs together.

As, to a tumultuous round of applause, the fly flew into the air, the kitchen door opened. It was Big Bob.

'Dad!' Bryony cried. 'Meet Mr Undrum, Man of Mystery. He's got transcendental powers, and he can bring things back to life!'

Big Bob took Ken's outstretched hand and shook it less than enthusiastically.

'Pleased to meet you,' he said, in a flat voice. Then, keeping hold of it, he turned and led the Man of Mystery over to the door.

'Perhaps Mr Undrum can show me his transcendental powers in the potting shed,' he said. 'Is he any good at making geraniums reappear?'

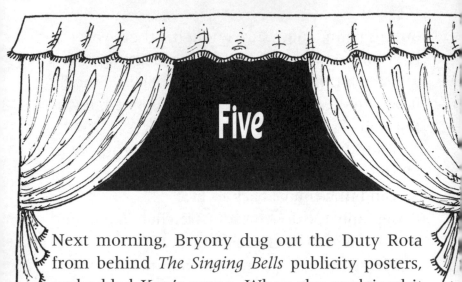

Five

Next morning, Bryony dug out the Duty Rota from behind *The Singing Bells* publicity posters, and added Ken's name. When she explained it to Ken, he told her he was more than happy to undertake all the duties and work his keep. It was, he said, the very least he could do in view of the Unfortunate Incident of Lily and the Geranium Cuttings.

So that Tuesday morning Bryony showed him the ropes, starting with the washing-up. As a nice froth built up in the sink, she bit the bullet.

'Could you teach me to do magic, Mr Undrum?' she asked. 'So's me and Abid could have a magic act?'

Ken smiled thoughtfully. Then he scooped up a handful of foam and clapped it between his hands gleefully, sending a shower of bubbles over them both.

'You betcha!' he exclaimed. 'You're bright as they come, Bryony. Let's give it a go!'

'Will you start by sawing-a-lady-in-half?'
Bryony asked, and to her delight Ken nodded.

'Brilliant, Mr Undrum!' she said, dusting the soapsuds off his sleeve and thinking again that Ken's wardrobe was in dire need of a makeover. 'I would so love to saw Abid in half!'

'Hold your horses,' laughed Ken. 'Need to learn how it's done first. You can do a lot of damage with a saw.'

Bryony drew a thoughtful little line through the soap suds.

'Maybe I could be a magician-on-wheels, Mr Undrum,' she said. 'Wouldn't that be slick?'

Ken smiled and nodded. Then he stared out of the kitchen window, suddenly absorbed in his own thoughts.

'A magician-on-wheels,' he muttered. 'My oh my, Ron would sure have loved that...'

Bryony pricked up her ears. There definitely was an American accent.

'Who's Ron, Mr Undrum?' she asked.

'No one,' he said softly. 'No one of any importance...'

And, eyes gleaming bright with a sudden strange sadness, he sploshed both hands into the washing-up bowl and scrubbed the milk jug till it shone.

* * *

That afternoon, as Bryony skated into the hall, a resounding 'Bang!' rang out from upstairs. Each of the star-studded bedroom doors flew open and the little 'uns rushed out. Bryony raced upstairs. As she neared the top, two rabbits tore past her and vanished. One of the rabbits was huge and determined-looking. Bryony's heart did a triple leap. Lily was at large once more.

Bryony pushed past the crowd of Bells and surveyed the scene. As she took in the horror of it all, her heart once more bled for Ken.

The bedroom looked like a bombsite. Just visible under an avalanche of boxes and hutches and pieces of mirrored box-side, the bed stood at a rakish angle. Shards of broken mirror covered the floor, and two of the hutch doors swung on their hinges. Each now contained just one rabbit.

In the midst of it all, his saw dangling from one hand, Ken stood gazing forlornly at the wreckage.

'Seven years bad luck,' he moaned. 'Seven years for each mirror, and there were four mirrors, so that makes...'

He paused and counted on his fingers. But his calculations were interrupted by a furious yell.

'Twenty-eight years!' Angelina roared. 'What on earth did you do with that saw, Mr Undrum?'

Ken looked down at the leg of the bed. It was sawn clean through.

'Thought it was a bit sticky,' he said miserably. 'Must have forced it.' And he began to pick up some of the pieces of glass.

'Be careful, Mr Undrum,' Bryony said, shooing the little 'uns away. 'We'll get a brush and do it carefully.'

Angelina followed Bryony into her room and as she took her Vipers off she stood at the door, her toe drumming against the pink shagpile.

'It seems to me, Bryony Bell,' she said, 'that you don't want *The Singing Bells* to succeed.'

Bryony looked up, truly horrified by the accusation.

'But, Angelina,' she protested, 'I'm your biggest fan.'

Angelina raised her eyebrows.

'That's what you say,' she said loftily. 'But I reckon you're out to sabotage the Summer Panto. Bringing that tenth-rate magician into the house...' Her braids rattled furiously together. 'Just because you didn't get a part,' she added, her nose in the air.

Bryony stood up. 'Honestly, Angelina, that's not true,' she implored. 'I only told Mr Undrum he could stay because he'd nowhere to go. I promise I'll keep an eye on him from now on.'

'OK,' said Angelina, sounding unconvinced.

'But I'm warning you – if one more thing happens, Mr Undrum's out – understood?'

And she marched off.

All that evening, as Bryony and Clarissa helped Ken clear up his room and Big Bob repaired his bed, the search for the runaway rabbits went on. But by nightfall no one had seen hide nor hair of them.

Bryony took Ken a comforting cup of cocoa.

'Don't worry, Mr Undrum,' she said, perching rather gingerly on his bed. 'Dad says he'll make you a new box in Antique Pine. It'll be safer than glass. And Lily's sure to turn up.'

'Don't know that she will, Bryony,' Ken said mournfully. 'Once Lily's heard the call of the wild, there's no stopping her. And she's on the run with Snowflake, and, well…' he blushed into his cocoa, 'boys will be boys – if you catch my drift.'

Bryony let it sink in, then nodded. 'Oh well,' she said at last, 'I suppose you can never have too many white rabbits.'

She bent down to pick up a piece of paper. As she handed it to Ken, she turned it over. Two rather faded young men, with identical handlebar moustaches smiled proudly out at her. On their shoulders, their wings pressed very closely together, sat dozens and dozens of white doves.

The smaller of the men looked familiar. 'Is this you, Mr Undrum?' Bryony asked.

'In my hey-day, Bryony,' Ken said, and his eyes gleamed like dark little spotlights. 'When we were on Broadway.'

'Broadway?' Bryony gasped. 'You were on Broadway?'

Broadway. There it was again! And the way Ken said it, with that American accent and the light in his eyes, made the very name sparkle.

She looked at the taller man. 'And who's this?' she asked.

A shadow passed over Ken's face. 'That's Ron,' he said.

Bryony opened her mouth to ask 'Who's Ron?' then, remembering the sad faraway look she had seen in Ken's eyes when they had washed the dishes together, closed it again.

'The doves are knock-out, Mr Undrum,' she said instead. 'Did you make them appear from out of your hats?'

As soon as she had said it, Bryony saw the light in Ken's eyes go out. Ken took the photograph gently but firmly out of her hand.

'I would be very grateful,' he said politely, 'if you would never, ever mention doves. It is a very sore subject.

'I seem to put a jinx on everyone I meet,' he went on miserably. 'I'm sure you must be wishing you hadn't invited me to stay.'

'Not a bit of it, Mr Undrum,' Bryony said, patting him on the shoulder. 'You're a great help, and soon you'll be teaching me magic too.' She paused. 'But…' she said slowly, '…we *will* have to be really careful from now on…'

Then she brightened up. 'Come on, Mr Undrum,' she said, 'what's that song you always sing to the rabbits?'

Ken gave a bright smile, and his moustache bristled with his usual cheerfulness.

'There's a rainbow round the corner,' he sang lustily,

'And a sky of blue above…'

When he had finished he leapt up and gave Bryony a very flamboyant bow.

'Nothing like the old songs to cheer you up!' he said, straightening up.

Bryony gave him a hug. 'Tomorrow'll be hunky-dory, you'll see,' she said, and Ken nodded brightly.

'Hunky-dory,' he repeated. 'That's what it'll be!'

But when Wednesday dawned, 'hunky-dory' was the very last thing it was.

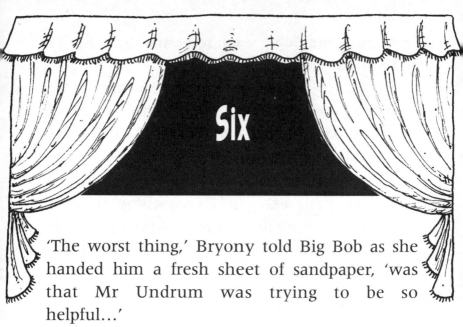

Six

'The worst thing,' Bryony told Big Bob as she handed him a fresh sheet of sandpaper, 'was that Mr Undrum was trying to be so helpful...'

It was Wednesday lunchtime, and Bryony had skated home lightning-fast to give Big Bob a hand with Ken's new Antique Pine 'sawing-a-lady-in-half' box.

'He means well,' Big Bob agreed, 'but there ain't two ways about it – your Mr Undrum's accident-prone. Specially around animals.'

For a while they sanded in silence, reliving the events of that terrible morning...

* * *

Ken, desperate to make amends, had risen at dawn, plodded round the garden calling 'Lily! Snowflake! Come home, all is forgiven!', fed the remaining rabbits, and cleaned the kitchen 'til it sparkled. Then he set the table and checked the time. Singing practice would not begin for at least an hour. It was far too early to start the toast and boiled eggs.

Then, as he was setting Clarissa's breakfast tray, he had an idea. Wouldn't it be nice to give all the Bells breakfast in bed? Make 'em feel like real stars, and more than make up for the day before. Delighted by his brainwave, he looked around for more trays and, finding nothing suitable, remembered the pile of Antique Pine planks in the potting shed waiting to be assembled into the new 'sawing-a-lady-in-half' box.

A tad narrow, Ken thought but, with careful handling and the addition of a nice paper doily or two, they would do the trick. He picked up five of them, (Little Bob, he decided, was too young to appreciate the gesture, and Big Bob could share Clarissa's) and headed back to the kitchen. He laid each plank with a bowl of cereal, a thickly buttered and strawberry-jammed slab of bread, and a mug of tea. Then, humming happily, he went out into the garden to pick roses to adorn each of the Bells' breakfasts.

And it was at that moment that Lily and Snowflake decided to come home.

Like two white tornadoes, the rabbits bounded past Ken and into the kitchen. Ken tore after them, but he was too late. Driven to a frenzy by the combined scents of six bowls of

Krispy Flakes and six thick layers of strawberry jam, Lily and Snowflake leapt on to the table and hopped ecstatically from Antique Pine plank to Antique Pine plank. Their whiskers had never trembled, nor their noses ever wobbled, so excitedly, as they settled their bottoms into the bowls of cereal and licked every drop of jam off the bread.

Then, once the slices were only slightly tacky, they turned round and, sitting on them, proceeded to demolish the Krispy Flakes. Finally, they nudged the mugs of tea onto the floor, where they smashed and spread their contents all over the kitchen.

For a while, Ken stared helplessly at the scene. Then, suddenly galvanised into action, he made a lunge at Lily and pinned her to his chest. But Lily had got the taste for Krispy Flakes. She clawed him furiously before jumping clear, leaving his face streaked with a mixture of blood and strawberry jam to which adhered two pink roses and a crumpled doily.

To make matters even worse, the first little Bell to get up to practise her scales was Angelina. On her way downstairs she had almost completed one octave – 'Doh, ray, me, fah, soh, lah, tee…' and, on the second last note, opened the kitchen door to find a warm wave of it lapping over her toes.

'…d-d-doh!' she stuttered as she gazed disbelievingly at the pile of jam-smeared, cereal-stuck Antique Pine planks.

And in the midst of it all Lily and Snowflake gazed innocently back at her, before returning to their breakfasts.

* * *

Bryony stopped sanding.

'*You* don't think I brought Mr Undrum here to sabotage the Summer Panto?' Bryony asked anxiously. ''Cause I didn't. I wanted to help him out, and I really want him to stay and teach me to be a magician!'

Big Bob stroked Bryony's head soothingly.

''Course you didn't want to sabotage the panto, Bryony,' he said softly. 'You meant well, just like Ken. But you've got to admit, lass – it isn't working.

'I had a talk with Angelina after breakfast,' he went on, 'and she's agreed that this morning's fiasco was a nice gesture gone wrong, but …' He sighed and ran his hand over the surface of the 'sawing-a-lady-in-half' box, '…it's like living with a time-bomb, having Ken here. Life with Ken Undrum,' he added, reaching for a cloth and a tin of furniture wax, 'sure ain't humdrum! Come on, Bryony – let's polish his box till it shines. We could all do with a bit of gloss today.'

Bryony copied Big Bob's little circular movements. When the surface was covered with wax, they buffed it up. Soon, the Antique Pine gleamed.

'Can we stick some silver stars on?' Bryony asked.

'Sure,' Big Bob smiled. 'Mind you,' he added, 'I don't think Ken's on the road to stardom. Shame to say it, but I reckon he's had his day.'

Bryony thought about this. The photo of the young men with their doves flashed into her mind again.

'I wonder about Mr Undrum, Dad,' she said slowly. 'I think he was once a big Broadway star. But then things went wrong somehow.'

She gave the box an extra-hard rub. She could almost see her red poppy hair-ties reflected in its surface now. But nothing was clear. It was still a blur…

'I keep asking him things,' she went on, 'and he starts to tell me, and then he stops. Doesn't he trust me?'

Big Bob rubbed his little brown moustache. 'Sometimes,' he said, 'telling's not so easy …' He sat down and patted his knees. Bryony perched on his lap, resting a hand on his bald patch to balance herself.

'I'll tell you a secret,' he whispered. 'A secret only your mum knows.' He gave Bryony a squeeze. ''Cause I know you'll keep it to yourself, and it'll maybe make it easier for you to understand Ken.'

'It's safe with me, Dad,' Bryony said gravely.

Big Bob took a big breath in. 'When I first set eyes on your mum,' he began, 'she was singing in the Pig and Whistle.' He gazed into the distance. *Smoke Gets in Your Eyes*, the song was, and to this day it brings me out in goosebumps to hear it.

'Anyway, I knew right off she was the girl for me. But I couldn't bring myself to ask her for a date – her being a singer and me just an apprentice joiner. So I did a very wrong thing.'

He looked up at Bryony. 'A very, very wrong thing,' he repeated. 'I told her a lie to impress her. I told her I was an airline pilot.'

'An airline pilot? You?' Bryony spluttered. 'You get dizzy up a ladder and you've never flown in your life!'

Big Bob blushed. 'I know, I know,' he said. 'But love makes fools of all of us, Bryony.'

'So – did she believe you?'

'Sure did. And she was impressed, and she let me take her to the pictures. But then she kept wanting to see me in my uniform, and somehow what had started out as a little lie started to grow bigger and bigger...'

In the distance a clock chimed. It was time to go back to school. Reluctantly Bryony got up, took both Big Bob's hands, and skated down the path pulling him after her.

At the gate she stopped. 'How did you get out of it, Dad?' she asked.

'Chocolate-covered fondant creams,' Big Bob smiled coyly.

Bryony gave him a quizzical look.

'Six juicy fruit flavours, in a gold box with a red lining. Cost me a packet. And,' he added, giving Bryony a push in the direction of school, 'I owned up.

'"I am only a humble joiner, Clarissa," I said, "but I give you my awl." And she said that was very clever. She also said she preferred a man with both feet on the ground. And then she ate the chocolate-covered fondant creams, and the rest is history.'

Bryony freewheeled backwards. 'Oh, Dad,' she sighed, 'that *is* romantic.'

She pirhouetted round Big Bob. 'Not quite sure what it's got to do with Ken though…'

Big Bob swivelled round too. 'Sometimes,' he explained, rotating on the ball of his foot, 'there are things in our past we don't want to tell. And, if we are going to tell them, we need to wait 'til the right moment.

'But if we do tell,' he said, stopping and swaying slightly, 'it's often a weight off our mind.' He clutched his head and staggered. 'So just ease up on Ken, lass. If he wants to tell, he'll do it in his own good time.'

And he wended his way giddily back to the potting shed.

Bryony skated thoughtfully schoolwards. She could see Abid waving at her and she rushed towards him, bursting to tell him how good the 'sawing-a-lady-in-half' box was looking.

But Abid had bad news to tell. And, in a week full of bad news, his bad news was the daddy of them all.

Seven

Bryony clutched Abid's shoulders and gave him a steadying squeeze.

'Go back to the beginning and slow down,' she told him firmly. 'Rushing's only making you wheeze. You didn't say Angelina's been given a hundred lines and banned from school dinners for the rest of the week? You didn't?'

Abid coughed several times. Bryony watched him with growing horror.

'Tell me you're nodding 'cause you're coughing, Abid,' she said desperately, 'and not 'cause it's true?'

But there was no doubt about it. Abid was nodding.

'But Angelina never does anything wrong,' Bryony said, shaking her head in disbelief. "The Angel of Peachtree Primary" Mrs Quigg calls her. How on earth did it happen?'

Abid struggled for breath, his face an interesting shade of damson.

'Flies,' he croaked, before another wheeze took over.

'Flies?' Bryony repeated.

'The whole dining hall was full of them, Bryony,' Abid went on, flapping his hands around at the memory. 'Dozens of bluebottles, buzzing round everyone's heads and landing in their Eve's puddings.'

Suddenly Bryony's world went into slow motion. Time had faded that morning's kitchen scene to a terrible blur of tepid tea, sticky doilies, and what seemed like a roomful of white rabbits and screaming Angelinas, but somewhere in it all she remembered seeing her sister splash over to the fridge, take out her lunchbox, and flounce back out with it.

Except that *that* lunchbox hadn't been yellow, had it? *That* lunchbox had been orange...

Bryony drew in a long breath.

'Oh my goodness!' she said. 'She took...'

Her sentence was finished by a voice behind her that seemed to come from the very bowels of Hell.

'I took *Mr Undrum's* lunchbox!'

Turning to face her sister, Bryony braced herself. She had never seen Angelina so seethingly angry. Even her braids seemed electrically charged.

Bryony's voice was a strangled whisper. 'But why does Mr Undrum keep—' She stopped. Suddenly, she had an awful feeling she knew the answer. What had Big Bob said? Your Mr Undrum's accident-prone. 'Specially around animals…

Angelina, hands on hips, gave Bryony a dreadful stare. 'Why does Mr Undrum keep flies in a lunchbox in the fridge? you were about to ask, Bryony,' she repeated through clenched teeth. 'I'll tell you why…'

Grimly, eyes half-closed, she advanced, prodding Bryony with a forefinger in time to each word of her answer.

'So – that – they – get – cold,' she stabbed out.

'So – they – look – dead,' she jabbed again.

'So – they – wake – up – in – his – hands,' she went on.

She took Bryony by the shoulders. ''Cause your Mr Ken Undrum can't do magic at all,' she said. 'He wouldn't know transcendental powers if he met them in his soup.'

Then she headed off towards the school gate, pausing only to add disparagingly, 'Mr *Con*undrum, that's what he is. And I'm telling you, Bryony Bell – this time he's out!'

Abid, who had been watching the scene in awed silence, put a large arm round Bryony and led her into the playground where the last of the lines were straggling in.

'It's not the end of the world,' he pointed out reasonably.

'It kind of is,' Bryony said, dangerously close to tears. 'It's the end for poor Mr Undrum and Lily and Snowflake and goodness-knows-how-many other rabbits. It's the end of me being the slickest, most glamorous magician the world has ever known.'

She gave a long, sad, sniff before announcing solemnly, 'It is the end of my career in magic.' Then she looked at Abid and corrected herself. '*Our* career in magic.'

Abid bit his lip. He had been about to point out that as far as he was concerned, a career in magic was the very last career he would ever want and that he was, as she well knew, destined for accountancy or brain surgery; but when he saw Bryony's lip tremble and her blue eyes fill with tears, his heart melted.

'It's not,' he said, as they trailed along to the classroom. ''Cause I've had a breathtakingly brilliant, scintillatingly surefire gem of an idea for once!'

Bryony gazed at him.

'Really?' she said, a little doubtfully.

Abid nodded, but before he could divulge the breathtakingly brilliant, scintillatingly surefire gem of an idea, Mrs Ogilvie, their teacher, glared out at them from behind a sheaf of Spelling Tests.

'Do take your time, Bryony and Abid,' she said with heavy irony. 'No pressure at all...'

Bryony and Abid, suitably chastened, slunk into their seats, sat up as brightly as they could manage, and prepared to give the day's Top Ten Spelling their best shots. Just as Bryony was carefully writing the last word, and wondering whether 'anomynous' *was* a word, Abid slid a note across the desk.

When she read it, Bryony's spirits soared.

Mr U. can stay with us.
Sounded Mum out yesterday. A OK.

'What about your asthma?' Bryony hissed. 'You know the rabbits are set to multiply?'

'All part of the Plan,' Abid grinned. 'They can live in the conservatory. It's like the Amazon rainforest in there. The damp'll stop hairs spreading through the house.'

'Are you sure, Abid?' Bryony said, hardly daring to believe her ears. 'Can you and your mum and dad cope with all Mr Undrum's props and...' she hesitated '...little ways?'

But Abid had become very serious. 'We can't throw him out on the street at his age,' he said. 'We'd never sleep easy again.'

Then he looked even more serious. 'There's just one thing worries me, Bryony,' he said. 'He hasn't got birds, has he? 'Cause you know feathers make me wheeze more than anything else.' He shuddered. 'I only have to think of that Swan costume you rescued me from, and it starts.'

Bryony thought back to the Ugly Duckling play. Abid had wheezed his way through the Swan role until they had persuaded Mrs Quigg to let her take over. Then, safely offstage, he had entranced the whole school as he sang the Swan song while Bryony skated.

'Don't worry,' she assured him. 'Not only does Mr Undrum not work with birds, he's got a thing about them too.' She lowered her voice confidentially. 'You're never to mention doves.'

Then she sat down on the pavement, changed

into her old black skates, and led the way home.

'Hurry up!' she called back to Abid. 'We need to be there when Angelina breaks the news about the flies. It could get very ugly…'

But when they reached Bryony's house, it was clear that word of Angelina's punishment had already reached home, for the pavement was piled high with bags, crates and rabbit hutches, the 'sawing-a-lady-in-half' box towering magnificently over everything. It had been decorated with silver stars, which somehow added an extra poignancy. Beside it all stood Mr Undrum, bidding Clarissa a tearful farewell.

'Think no more of it, dear lady,' he said, his voice muffled by a large red handkerchief. 'It's always happening…'

'I'm sorry, Ken,' Clarissa said, 'but we must consider Angelina's feelings. She's devastated.'

She pushed an envelope into Ken's hand. 'Back wages for all the housework,' she explained gently. 'Tide you over 'til you find somewhere.'

Ken looked about to protest, but Clarissa said firmly, 'Angelina insisted. Because of Lily's condition, you know. Loves rabbits, does our Angelina. Always did.'

Ken thanked Clarissa gratefully. Then he glanced sideways, to see Bryony's smiling face.

'It'll be fine,' he said, forcing a little smile too.

'You know what they say – don't you, Bryony?'

'Sure, Mr Undrum,' Bryony said promptly. '"There's a rainbow round the corner..."'

As Ken solemnly joined in, she did three joyous pirhouettes, finishing up facing Abid.

'And this, Mr Undrum,' she said, 'is Abid Ashraf – your very own personal rainbow!'

'Mr Undrum,' Abid said formally, 'my parents and I would be happy to offer you and your pets accommodation until circumstances improve...' and was engulfed by a rapturous Ken and Clarissa who thanked him 'from the very depths of their souls'.

While Abid recovered his breath, Bryony skated thoughtfully round the pile of props. She gave the 'sawing-a-lady-in-half' box a gentle stroke.

A burning question was on her lips – and it wasn't going to be long before she had her answer.

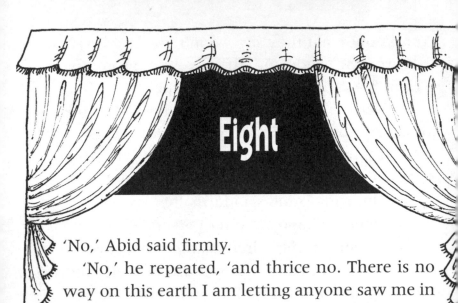

Eight

'No,' Abid said firmly.

'No,' he repeated, 'and thrice no. There is no way on this earth I am letting anyone saw me in half. Even you, Bryony.'

It was Saturday morning, and they were in the marble hall of Abid's house. Ken was upstairs being measured for a new cloak; the rabbits were revelling in the steamy warmth of the conservatory, and Bryony, her Viper 3000s white and gleaming, was skating round the 'sawing–a-lady-in-half' box, savouring the wonderful smoothness of the floor. Her Swan costume, which she had donned in preparation for Ken's first lesson in magic, felt as graceful and as feathery as she remembered. The very air sparkled with magic.

'But, Abid, you have to!' Bryony protested. 'Your mum's even gone to the bother of unpicking the swan from my bodice and embroidering on a silver star so I match the box.'

She peered into the varnished surface, now so glossy she could see the silver stars on her hair-ties. Her disappointment reflected back at her.

'I get claustrophobia, Bryony,' Abid said miserably. 'That's a fear of confined spaces.' He sighed. 'And you don't get more confined than an Antique Pine box.'

From upstairs a door opened and Ken, led proudly by Mrs Ashraf, descended and gave his cloak a stately whirl. Then, kissing Mrs Ashraf's elegantly manicured fingers, he struck a pose against one of the marble pillars.

'Oh, Mr Undrum!' Bryony gasped. 'You look a million dollars!' She pulled out the cloak to admire its shimmering, kingfisher-blue lining.

'Careful, sweetie,' Mrs Ashraf said, 'it's only tacked. And of course, it still has silver-sequined stars to come.'

'It's just what the act needs,' Ken said, giving Mrs Ashraf a stiff little bow. 'A new gloss, a new polish…'

'A couple of new magicians,' Bryony added.

Ken clicked his heels together and nodded, and she clasped her hands in rapture.

'Today I will initiate you both into the secrets of magic,' he announced importantly. 'Come along, young man – hop in!'

Abid winced.

'I'd just as soon not be initiated, Mr Undrum,' he said, shooting his mother a desperate glance. 'I don't think Mum would want me being sawn in half. Would you, Mum?'

Bryony bit her lip. 'It's only a trick,' she assured Mrs Ashraf. 'I won't actually cut him.'

Mrs Ashraf pushed Abid towards the box. 'Of course it's only a trick!' she said. 'Now, Abid, don't be a big baby. After all Bryony's done for you…'

There was a scuffle as Ken and Mrs Ashraf manouevred Abid in, then banged down the lid

Abid, his feet sticking out of two holes at the bottom of the box and his head protruding from the other end, looked like a terror-stricken turtle.

'What about my claustrophobia?' he wailed, rolling his eyes. But Bryony's mind was on higher things. Ken had handed her the saw and the wand.

'Ooooooh, Mr Undrum,' she breathed. 'It's like my whole arm's vibrating with magic power.'

'Not y-y-your sawing hand, B-b-bryony?' Abid stopped moaning long enough to stutter. 'Oh please let me out...'

Ignoring him, Ken pointed to the groove round the box's middle. 'Now, Bryony,' he said, 'this is where you start sawing. Breathe in, Abid.' He rocked Bryony's hand gently back and forth. The saw sliced through the groove as easily as a knife cuts butter.

'Bravo, Bryony!' Ken cheered. 'A joiner's daughter through and through.'

Abid, who had now turned an unhealthy yellowish-white and appeared to have lost the power of speech, appealed silently to his mother, but Mrs Ashraf spun round on her pointed little heels.

'It's like this when we go to the dentist, Bryony,' she said, floating off into the living room. 'He's much worse when I'm around.'

Ken now turned his attention to Abid. 'Pay attention, young man,' he said, 'otherwise we could end up with blood on the carpet, so to speak.'

Bryony watched Abid's face with interest. At the mention of the word 'blood' he sucked in his cheeks and turned grey. She tried to concentrate on the wand and the magic words Ken was going to teach her, but it was no use.

'You are all right, aren't you?' she said, feeling Abid's brow. It was cold and clammy.

'I don't want to let you down, Bryony,' Abid intoned, eyes tightly shut, 'but I so hate it in here.'

'It's no use,' Bryony told Ken with a sigh. 'We'll have to swap.'

Regretfully she opened the lid, hauled Abid out and handed him the saw and the wand. 'Right, Abid,' she said, hopping into the box herself. 'You're the magician, I'm the glamorous assistant – get sawing!'

Abid steeled himself and placed the saw into the groove. It shuddered, then stuck.

'OK,' said Ken, 'this is where it gets really clever. Abid – take the saw out, wave the wand and say some magic words. Give Bryony enough time to raise her tummy up to the top of the box.' He glanced at Bryony. 'Think you can manage that, Bryony?'

'No problem at all, Mr Undrum,' Bryony assured him. 'And when Abid starts sawing again, he puts the saw in below my bottom - isn't that it?'

Ken nodded. 'Spot on, Bryony!' They both looked at Abid expectantly.

'Come on,' said Bryony. 'It's really uncomfortable lying here with my tummy in the air.'

Abid hesitated. 'I'm scared there's bits of you still hanging down,' he gulped.

'I'm fine,' Bryony groaned impatiently. 'Do get on with it!'

Abid had three goes at pushing in the saw. Finally he stopped, wiped the sweat off his brow, and to everyone's surprise announced, 'I've just thought what Mrs Quigg would do.'

Bryony's tummy dropped in astonishment. 'What in heaven's name has Mrs Quigg got to do with it?'

'Well,' Abid went on, 'remember that song she taught us about whistling a happy tune whenever we feel afraid?'

Bryony raised her eyebrows to the ceiling and nodded.

'That's what I'll do, if you've no objections, Mr Undrum,' he went on. 'Only I'll sing rather than whistle, and I'll fit in magic words too.'

Ken shrugged. 'Sing away,' he said. 'Whatever helps.'

Abid looked over at Bryony. 'Ready?' he asked.

'Bottom's up,' Bryony winked. Then she lay back and listened to Abid's soprano voice as, suddenly transformed, he pushed the saw back and forth below her as confidently as if he had been doing it all his life, and, from the sidelines, Ken watched with growing delight.

Abracadabra, kalamazoo, Abid sang as he sawed,
   Watch as the lady is cut in two.
   Abracadabra, kalamazee,
   Be truly ASTOUNDED at what you see.

The saw had gone as far as it could, and Abid withdrew it. Carefully he eased the two halves of the box a few centimetres apart, hissed,

70

'Wiggle your toes!' to Bryony, who smiled broadly and obliged, then went on singing:

Abracadabra, kalamazoh,
Watch as she wiggles her sawn-off toe.
Abracadabra, kalamzick,
It really IS magic, it isn't a trick!

With a grin at Bryony he gave the saw a final flourish, sang the last verse of his song, and bowed low:

What is our secret? No one can tell!
And now let us hear it…
For ASHRAF AND BELL!

Bryony erupted out of the box and skated round to give Abid a huge pat on the back. 'That was wicked, Abid!' she told him. 'Wasn't it, Mr Undrum?'

Ken shook Abid's hand warmly. 'You have a beautiful voice,' he said, 'and great stage presence, young man.'

'Have I really?' Abid said uncertainly. 'I never think I have…

'It's just that … well … Bryony always looks after me. Like when there are fights at school.' He gazed lovingly at Bryony. 'I'd do anything for her,' he concluded.

'Except anything to do with birds,' he added, after a pause.

At the mention of the word 'birds' Bryony looked anxiously at Ken. Sure enough, his little shoulders were sagging.

'Mr Undrum?' she said. 'Are you all right?'

Ken put a hand on Bryony's arm. Then, motioning to them both to follow him, he led the way silently upstairs to his room. He patted the bed, and Bryony sat down on one side and Abid on the other.

'The time has come,' Ken told them, 'to tell you my story.' And Abid and Bryony each placed a comforting arm on his shoulders.

'I too had someone who always looked after me,' Ken said sadly. 'But something went very, very wrong.

'It began fifty years ago. On Broadway. With Ron, and the American flag, and fifty white doves...'

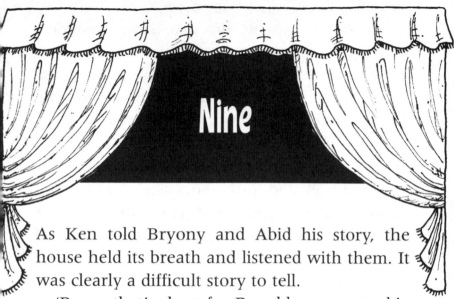

Nine

As Ken told Bryony and Abid his story, the house held its breath and listened with them. It was clearly a difficult story to tell.

'Ron – that's short for Ronaldo – was my big brother,' Ken began. 'He always fought my battles.

'We hadn't two dimes to rub together, so Ron and me decided we'd set up as a magic act. Work our way up through the New York clubs – make it big on Broadway!' He laughed ruefully. 'It's what everyone dreams of, isn't it, Bryony?'

'Broadway or bust, Mr Undrum,' she agreed softly.

'And you know,' Ken went on, 'we darn near made it.' His eyes sparkled with sudden delight. 'We were good! Well ... Ron was good. Didn't matter what Ron tried, he made it big...'

For a moment a smile lingered on his face. Then it disappeared again.

'What happened then?' Bryony asked.

'We finally got the big Broadway audition,' Ken said. 'And what an act we had planned!'

He jumped off the bed. 'Picture it,' he said, reaching up and spreading his arms wide, 'the American flag – the Stars 'n' Stripes – bigger than this room! We sank every dollar we had into making it, and it was awesome.' He swept his hand back and forth above their heads. 'The background was red tinsel, the stripes were a coupla hundred blue bulbs that flashed on and off, and the stars...'

Ken stopped, overcome with emotion.

'What were the stars, Mr Undrum?' Abid asked.

When Ken managed to speak, his voice was barely audible.

'Fifty white doves,' he said.

Bryony shot a look at Abid.

'Fifty?' she asked.

Ken nodded. 'Yup,' he said. 'Number of stars on the ol' Stars 'n' Stripes. ''Course you didn't see them to start with. That was the trick.'

'You made fifty doves appear by magic?' Bryony asked, incredulously.

'We'd show the audience this empty box,' Ken nodded. 'Open all the doors – you know the kinda thing. Then there'd be a drum roll, Ron would wave his wand and at the same time I would lift the lid and out they'd fly!'

Ken's eyes sparkled again, like dark little diamonds, as he gazed up towards the ceiling. With a worried frown, Abid followed his gaze, almost expecting to see fifty doves peering down from the cornicing.

''Specially trained, they were,' Ken went on. 'I tell you – it was phenomenal.'

'Well, it *would have been* phenomenal,' he corrected himself, 'if I hadn't messed up big-time.'

'Messed up?' Bryony asked.

'Always had a jinx around livestock,' Ken nodded. 'Even in those days. There was a crate under the stage where the doves were hidden, and I'd move a catch with my toe to open it. Then out would fly the doves, up into the magic box, so when I opened the lid – Lift off!'

Ken raised both hands, making a gesture like a rocket going into orbit.

'Except they didn't,' he said, bringing his hands back down. 'On our big night I kicked the catch, opened the lid, and nothing happened. Just a bit of squawking and a few feathers...'

'Why, Mr Undrum?' asked Abid.

'Set the catch wrong, didn't I,' Ken said, a vein pulsing on his temple. 'Flaming doves were stuck. Took us two days to get them out and when we did, the smell would've knocked you sideways!'

Ken buried his face in his hands. 'Our Broadway career,' he sobbed, 'in ruins. And all because of my incompetence. Just like I did at your house, Bryony – messed everything up for *The Singing Bells* and now they'll never forgive me.'

He took his red handkerchief out of his pocket and wiped his brow.

'Of course,' he continued, 'Ron was livid. 'You are an albatross around my neck, Ken!' he said. And then he marched off, set up on his own, and I've never seen him since.'

Ken gave his nose three hearty blows. 'Still can't get a whiff of pigeon droppings,' he said, 'but I think of Ronaldo…'

For a while no one spoke. Then Abid did. 'Mr Undrum,' he said. 'Do you know where Ron is?'

Ken nodded. 'Runs a big Broadway theatre. They call him "The Great Ronaldo" now.'

At the words 'Broadway theatre', Bryony sat bolt upright.

'Maybe,' she said slowly, 'if you met him again, he'd help you, like in the old days?'

But Ken stood up. 'Nope,' he said, taking off his cloak and giving it a resolute swipe. 'It ain't right, expecting someone to fight your battles for you.' He lay back on the bed and closed his eyes.

Abid cleared his throat. 'I disagree, Mr Undrum,' he said quietly. 'I let Bryony fight my battles.'

Ken turned his back on them. 'I said nope,' he repeated. 'And 'nope' is what I darn well mean.'

Unabashed, Bryony tugged his shirt hard. 'Mr Undrum!' she shouted. 'We won't take nope for an answer.'

There was still no movement. Bryony appealed to Abid, who lifted a few locks of russet hair and whispered the magic words into Ken's ear.

'I let Bryony fight my battles,' he said simply, ''cause Bryony wins battles.'

Then, as Ken rolled round to face him, Abid added, in a perfect American accent, 'Sometimes, Mr Undrum, a man's gotta do what a man's gotta do...'

* * *

Bryony skated slowly home. All in all, she reflected, it had been a good day. She had been sawn in half; Ken had contacted his brother; and, best of all, the magic duo *Ashraf and Bell – Magic on Wheels* – had been born.

After Abid's masterstroke, it had been easy to wheedle Ken round. They had found The Great Ronaldo's website, and Ken had sent him an e-mail. Now all they could do was wait.

As she neared home, the sound of *The Singing Bells* wafted out on the spring air and Bryony poked her head through the Music Studio door. The sight she saw brought tears of pride to her eyes.

On the stage, Melody and Melissa and Emmy-Lou, wearing sugar-pink tap shoes and pink satin leotards, stood watching Clarissa expectantly. Little Bob, encased in a pink sequined babygrow and almost hidden by a big drum, was beating a steady rhythm and gurgling 'Bobway or bust!' in time with it. In the wings, Bryony could see Angelina waiting nervously. And when she saw how she was dressed, she drew a long admiring breath in through her teeth.

Clarissa tapped the fluorescent pink music stand with her baton. 'Fairy Godmother number – take six!' she announced. 'I'm telling you,' she murmured to Bryony as she came in, 'if there's a Broadway headhunter at the Empress, it's our heads he's going to hunt – sure as eggs!'

Then she pointed her baton at the chorusline, and they began, very slowly and quietly, to sing:

If your dress is needing changing
Or your pumpkin re-arranging
Or you want your mice turned into
something N-I-C-E...

As they held the last notes in a melodious chord, Clarissa pointed the baton at Little Bob, who banged his drum exactly in time to her mouthed words:

...two, three, FOUR...

On the last beat, Angelina made her entrance. And what an entrance it was! In the history of Fairy Godmothers, Bryony thought, there had never been a Fairy Godmother with as much style as Angelina Bell. Her catsuit was so white and frostily sparkling, she looked as though she had been dipped in sugar. Her braids were pinned up with dozens of tiny golden stars, and she had wings that shimmered like mother-of-pearl.

Best of all, she carried a large, glittery, star-topped wand, and when she saw it, Bryony almost drooled. That was what a wand should look like!

Backed by Melody, Melissa and Emmy-Lou, and ably accompanied by Little Bob on drum,

Angelina kicked her feet in the air and launched into her show-stopping number:

Beat the drum! for the Fairy Godmother
Light the lights! 'Cause there's really no other
She'll transform you if you'll let her…
She can change things
for the b-e-t-t-e-r…

On cue from Clarissa, Little Bob beat his drum more slowly. Melody, Melissa and Emmy-Lou, linking arms, began a series of high kicks during which they rotated to finish on one knee, arms outstretched towards Anglina. And Angelina, basking in glory, stood centre stage waving her wand solemnly to and fro.

'Bravo!' said Clarissa. 'Just watch the way you wave the wand though, Angelina. You're changing a pumpkin into a coach – not serving at Wimbledon.'

Bryony jumped onto the stage where she patted Little Bob on the head and shook Melody and Melissa and Emmy-Lou heartily by the hand. Then, the past forgotten in a haze of sisterly love and professional admiration, she skated towards Angelina, arms outstretched.

But the hug never came. As Bryony approached her, Angelina side-stepped and swept past her.

'I can not forgive you,' she said haughtily. 'The flies were the last straw. The flies were unforgivable.'

And she marched offstage, poking her head back through the curtains to add, 'I will never speak to you again, Bryony Bell. As long as I live.'

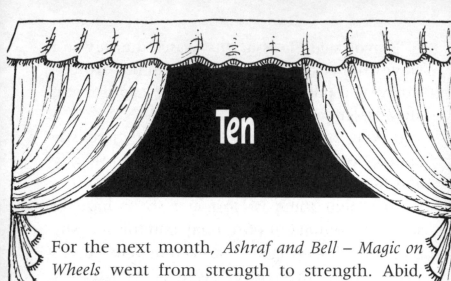

Ten

For the next month, *Ashraf and Bell – Magic on Wheels* went from strength to strength. Abid, ably assisted by Bryony, became adept at the 'Bread-on-a-Thread' trick and even developed a method of singing with his mouth full which made it doubly impressive.

Bryony excelled at producing rabbits from a hat, and Abid's confidence in sawing her in half soared to giddy heights. To cap it all, Mrs Ashraf made him a silk salwar kameez with a peacock-feather pattern which he wore with a gold lamé turban to great magical effect.

But best of all, The Great Ronaldo responded to Ken's e-mail. By chance, he was just about to go on a UK tour and agreed to make the Empress Theatre his first stop to watch the new magic act.

The only fly in the ointment was Angelina. For four weeks, despite Bryony's best efforts at a truce, not one word had passed between them. Bryony was hurt to the quick.

* * *

It was Saturday – the day of The Great Ronaldo's arrival. No one in Bryony's family, not even Big Bob, knew about it.

'Come along, everyone!' Clarissa shouted over the breakfast table. 'Music Studio for Singing Practice – then rehearsal at the Empress!'

Little Bob bounced up and down in his high chair, drowning out everybody with his Bobway or busts. Taking his cue, Clarissa slapped her knees three times and led the whole family in a raucous rendering of the song. At the second chorus, Bryony heaved on her rucksack, laced up her Viper 3000s, and set off.

The Great Ronaldo was due to arrive at the Empress mid-morning, and Bryony was to meet Abid and Ken, with the magic equipment, there. When she skated in they had already set up the 'sawing-a-lady-in-half' box. It looked magnificent under the stage lights.

'Great!' breathed Bryony. 'And it's OK for us to use the stage?'

'No one's due for an hour,' Ken said. 'Mention The Great Ronaldo,' he winked, 'and the world's your oyster!'

Bryony and Abid exchanged looks. Ken was very pale and worried-looking.

'Ron wouldn't have said he'd come if he hadn't wanted to make it up, Mr Undrum,'

Bryony pointed out, but Ken remained unconvinced.

'Such a long time,' he kept muttering. 'So much ill-feeling...'

Eventually Bryony and Abid let him be and went to look out for The Great Ronaldo. He was easy to spot.

'Oh, Abid!' cried Bryony. 'Look at the car!'

A silver limousine purred to a halt and a white-uniformed chauffeur hopped out and held the door open for The Great Ronaldo. Never in their lives had Bryony and Abid seen anyone so rich and successful.

The Great Ronaldo was at least six-feet tall and broad as a barn door. He wore a black-and-white striped suit, a white fur coat draped across his enormous shoulders, and a black stetson that hid most of his jet-black hair. When he smiled at them through his enormous black moustache, the sun glinted off a dozen gold fillings. And when he stretched his hand out to shake theirs, every finger held a jewelled ring.

'You must be l'il ol' Bryony Bell,' he boomed as he pumped Bryony's arm up and down. Then he gave Abid a slap that knocked him off balance. 'And Ken's rainbow – Abid Ashraf. Sure am mighty pleased to make your acquaintance!'

Bryony, lost for words, led the way into the theatre.

Ahead, she could see Ken standing alone in the spotlight, eyes down and shoulders hunched.

Before Ron could stride onto the stage, Bryony pulled his coat. 'Mr Ronaldo,' she whispered, 'you know what my dad always says?'

Ron bent down. 'What does your dad always say, Bryony?' he asked.

'He always says you should let bygones be bygones,' Bryony said nervously.

Then she paused. A picture of Angelina flashed into her mind. 'Though it takes two to tango,' she added, 'which is what my mum always says.'

Ron straightened up, nodding. 'I reckon your dad's got the right idea, Bryony,' he said.

Then out on to the stage Ron walked, arms outstretched towards his little brother. Bryony glanced anxiously at Abid, but when she looked back Ron was hugging Ken so hard he raised him right off the ground, and when he finally put him down Bryony heard him say softly, 'Oh, Ken, Ken – why did we wait this long?'

* * *

'So,' said The Great Ronaldo, sitting astride a chair and wiping a last tear from his eye, 'you guys gonna let me see your act?'

He winked at Bryony and Abid. 'Never was a magician like my kid brother, you know,' he said, flashing a 20-carat smile at Ken. 'OK, so maybe things went a bit wrong sometimes…'

Ken blushed.

'…but that's water under the bridge, isn't it, Ken?' he finished. 'Gee – I just love the look of the new outfit. What're you calling yourselves?'

'*Ashraf and Bell – Magic on Wheels,*' Bryony said promptly. 'Mr Undrum is our manager. Abid does all the magic 'cept for the rabbits and sings the spells in a lovely soprano voice. And I'm the skating glamorous assistant.'

'And we're both dressed by none other than Shabana Ashraf, Designer to the Stars,' Abid put in, adding proudly, 'She's my mum.'

'Would you like to see Abid saw me in half, Mr Ronaldo?' Bryony offered. Ron nodded, and, without further ado, they performed their *tour de force* more slickly than ever before. When they had finished, every gold filling in Ron's mouth sparkled approval.

'Great star potential,' he beamed. 'I reckon I could make you big on Broadway.'

'Do you hear that, Bryony?' Abid breathed, looking at Bryony ecstatically.

But Bryony's mind, suddenly and unexpectedly, was elsewhere.

'Thank you very much, Mr Ronaldo,' she said politely, peering out into the auditorium. In the distance she could hear a gurgly little voice chanting breathlessly, 'It's Bobway or bust...'

All of a sudden, she pictured herself arriving in Broadway – the one and only Broadway Bell. Tears blurred her eyes.

'Here's the next act,' The Great Ronaldo said, getting up. 'Better be off...'

But Bryony held his arm. 'Just a minute, please,' she begged. She gazed out into the theatre's darkness. Her thoughts turned somersaults.

'Why did we wait so long?' Ron had said.

Fifty years, thought Bryony. They had waited fifty years to let bygones be bygones. Suddenly she had a vision of two old ladies, one with white braids and one with pert white bunches done up with forget-me-not hair-ties, meeting under a faraway stage spotlight, hugging each other, and saying just the same thing.

The Singing Bells had reached the stage now and Clarissa was leading the way up. Angelina, already dressed in her Fairy Godmother costume, pushed past Bryony.

'I might have known!' she screamed, giving Ken a withering look and hauling the 'sawing-a-lady-in-half' box off its stools. 'Bryony Bell messes things up yet again!'

'Allow me, young lady,' Ron said, as he lifted it onto his huge shoulders and carried it offstage. 'We won't delay you.'

Bryony sidled up to Clarissa. 'Quick, Mum!' she whispered. 'Do the Fairy Godmother number, and give it everything you've got!'

She winked at Clarissa and nodded in the direction of The Great Ronaldo.

'Mr Undrum's big brother,' she whispered. 'And Broadway's Mr Big!'

Leaving Clarissa open-mouthed she skated backstage, took Ron's arm, and settled him in the front row. Abid, meanwhile, collected Ken and deposited him beside his brother. When both men were settled and *The Singing Bells* in position, Bryony poked her head between Ron and Ken.

'Have a look at this,' she whispered, 'and tell me *they* don't have star potential, too!'

In Luigi's Pizza Parlour that afternoon, the biggest table in the house buzzed with Bells and Ashrafs. At its head The Great Ronaldo, whose treat it was, sat beside Ken, ordering pizzas the size of cartwheels for everyone.

Clarissa, her hair swept up into a luxurious creamy froth and her ruby earrings sparkling like tiny bright cherries, gazed incredulously at the Knickerbocker Glory Little Bob had just been given.

'Bobway or bust,' Little Bob muttered in a determined voice as he stood on his chair and dive-bombed the first layer of jelly with his spoon. Everyone raised their glasses and joined in, and Bryony, glowing with pride and happiness, nestled into Big Bob's side.

They both looked over at Angelina. 'Bryony could've gone to Broadway on her own, couldn't she, Angelina?' Big Bob said gently. 'You Broadway Bells've got her, and Mr Undrum, to thank!'

Angelina examined her pizza crust. Then, flicking her braids back off her face, she gave Bryony the tiniest of smiles.

Ron stood up. 'How many first-class tickets to Broadway then?' he asked, and all the Bells, except Big Bob, cheered and clapped and shouted 'Yee-hah!' at the very tops of their voices.

Bryony turned to her dad. 'Couldn't you come too?' she whispered, willing him to say 'yes'. 'Please?'

But Big Bob shook his head. 'You'll never get me on a plane, Bryony,' he said. 'You know that. And besides...' He nodded towards Ken, '...someone needs to stay at home just now, don't they?'

Bryony grinned. 'Oh yes, Dad – of course,' she said. 'Nearly forgot!' And she jumped off her chair and slipped out of the room.

When she came back, she was holding both hands in front of her with a bright-red silk scarf draped over them, and she wore a mysterious expression on her face. Pausing to wink at Big Bob, who winked back and whispered, 'Go for it, princess!' she walked slowly along the lines of silent people. Every eye in the place was on the shiny magical mound she carried. When she came to Angelina's place, she stopped.

Angelina put the rest of her pizza crust down. She looked at Bryony with just a tinge of suspicion, but Bryony continued unabashed. 'You got that brilliant Fairy Godmother wand with you, Angelina?' she asked.

Angelina nodded. She reached below the table and picked it up. 'Once the Summer Panto's over,' she said softly to Bryony, 'perhaps you'd like to have it? As a thank-you present for getting us an audition with The Great Ronaldo?'

Bryony's blue eyes sparkled with happiness. 'Love to, Angelina,' she said. 'That sure is a wand with attitude!' Then she held her red-silk-covered hands out to her sister. 'I reckon you can do magic too, Angelina,' she said, nodding toward the wand. 'What do you think?'

Angelina looked down at the silk scarf. Its surface was moving slightly, almost as if it were breathing. She looked at Big Bob, who raised his eyebrows and gave her a little nod.

'Go on,' urged Bryony. 'Abid'll tell you the magic words if you like.'

Angelina glanced over her shoulder to where Abid was grinning down at her. He bent and whispered the spell and when she heard it,

Angelina smiled shyly at Bryony. Then she waved her wand.

'Let bygones be bygones,' she repeated as, slowly and dramatically, she pulled the scarf away.

The whole table joined Angelina in a sigh of perfect happiness. Then everyone stood.

'Broadway or bust, and let bygones be bygones,' they chorused, as they raised their glasses to the sugar-white baby rabbit that quivered its tiny whiskers and hopped into Angelina's outstretched hand.

Then they sat down again. Only Big Bob remained standing, and he proposed another toast. 'To our princess, Bryony,' he said, tipping his glass of Newcastle Brown in Bryony's direction. 'The most magic Bell of all!'

About the Author

Franzeska G. Ewart was born in Stranraer – a small town by the sea in Galloway – and still likes to be there as often as she can. She loves the sea, the lochs, and the rivers. Most of the time, though, she lives in Glasgow where she has a part-time job teaching English as an Additional Language at Glendale Primary School.

When she's not writing she likes to read, draw, and listen to music. She loves to play music too and has recently joined the Scottish National Recorder Orchestra where she plays tenor and treble recorder. The Bryony books are fun to write because there's so much music in them, and they give her the chance to write lots of songs.

Franzeska has had over a dozen books for children published. These include *Speak Up Spike*, *Shadowflight* and *The Pen-pal from Outer Space* all of which were named Guardian Book of the Week.

About Under the Spell of Bryony Bell:

Franzeska also loves looking after her white cat, Lily. While she was writing *Under the Spell of Bryony Bell*, she decided to call one of Ken Undrum's white rabbits Lily too. She wanted Lily the cat to have kittens, so she decided that if she made Lily the rabbit have babies, it might bring Lily the cat luck – which indeed it did. Lily is now the proud mother of five kittens!

You can see Lily on Franzeska's website: www.alchemywebsite.com/franzeskaewart

Another fantastic Black Cat ...

FRANZESKA G. EWART
Bryony Bell
Tops the Bill

Bryony dreams of being a top-notch
skater. But she has to send back her new,
state-of-the-art skates to pay for her
sisters' costumes for *TV Family Star Turns*.
Poor Bryony. It's not much fun at school,
either. In the end of term play, she's cast
as the Ugly Ducking. Can the family's
fortunes – and Bryony's – turn in time
to give her the chance to strut her stuff?

Black Cats – collect them all!